Calculus

of a Single Variable

Seventh Edit